Honeypot Hill

To the City

Saffron Thimble's
Sewing Shop

The Orchards

Paddle Steamer
Quay

Aunt
Marigold's
General
Store

Lavender Valley
Garden Centre

Healing House and Garden

The Worthingtons' House

Lavender Lake

Bumble Bee's Teashop

Lavender Lake
School of Dance

SCHOOL

Hedgerows Hotel
Where Mimosa lives

Peppermint
Pond

Rosehip School

Summer Meadow

Christmas Corner

Wildspice Woods

Honeysuckle Cottage
Poppy's House

Forget-Me-Not Cottage
Grandpa's House and Office

Poppy Field

N
W   E
S

Honeypot Cottage
Honey and Granny Bumble's House

Blossom
Bakehouse

Cornsilk Castle
and Courtyard

Village Hall

Sage's
Vet Surgery

Post Office

Beehive
Beauty Salon

River Swan

Riverside
Stables

Barley Farm
The Meadowsweets' House

Honeypot Hill
Railway Station

To Camomile Cove
via Periwinkle Lane

THE PLAY
A PICTURE CORGI BOOK: 978 0 552 55761 0

First published in Great Britain by Picture Corgi, an imprint of Random House Children's Books
A Random House Group Company

This edition published 2008

1 3 5 7 9 10 8 6 4 2

Text copyright © Janey Louise Jones, 2006
Illustrations copyright © Picture Corgi Books, 2006
Design by Tracey Cunnell

Picture Corgi Books are published by Random House Children's Books, 61–63 Uxbridge Road, London W5 5SA

www.princesspoppy.com
www.rbooks.co.uk

Addresses for companies within the Random House Group Limited can be found at: www.randomhouse.co.uk/offices.htm

THE RANDOM HOUSE GROUP Limited Reg. No. 954009

A CIP catalogue record for this book is available from the British Library.

Printed in China

Princess Poppy

The Play

Written by Janey Louise Jones

PICTURE CORGI

For Ben, Ollie and Louis,
with maternal and eternal love

★

The Play

featuring

Mum
★

Princess Poppy

Honey
★

Daisy
★

Grandpa
★

Edward
★

"Mum, I'm bored," grumbled Poppy. "There's nothing to do here."

"Daisy and Edward will be here soon with Grandpa, and look, here comes Honey," said Mum as Poppy's best friend skipped towards them. "Maybe she'll be able to think of something to do."

"Hi, Poppy," called Honey. "What are you doing?"

"Nothing. I'm so bored," said Poppy. "My cousins are visiting today with Grandpa, but there's nothing to do. Can *you* think of anything?"

Honey sat down next to Poppy, and tried to think of something to do . . .

"I know," said Honey after a few minutes. "Let's put on a play!

Granny Bumble took me to see one in the city last summer — it was amazing because there were lots of fairies in it and everything looked really pretty, although I didn't understand all of it and it *was* quite long."

"Ooooh, that's a brilliant idea, Honey! I've always wanted to be in a play," said Poppy, "but we're going to need . . .

tickets . . .

costumes . . .

actors . . .

oh, and an actual story!"

"Hi, everyone!" called Poppy, as Grandpa and her cousins walked through the garden gate. "Guess what we're doing today?"

Before they even had a chance to reply Poppy started excitedly telling them about the play.

"There's so much to do, we need to start right now," she told them.

"What's the play about?" asked Grandpa.

"I'm not quite sure yet," replied Poppy. "I thought *you* might be able to help us to make up a story. It has to be about princesses, though. Edward can be my page boy . . ."

"But I want to be a wizard or a pirate!" protested Edward.

"Well you can't," said Poppy. "It's *my* play!"

"Stop squabbling and leave it to me!" said Grandpa, as he settled down in his deckchair, holding a notebook and pen.

"Edward, you clear all my toys away so there's lots of room," said Poppy. "You make tickets, Honey, and hand them out to everyone in Honeypot Hill. And Daisy, you can go and get the dressing-up chest and make-up box from my room."

They all sprang into action, except Poppy . . .

She put on her big straw sun-hat, sat down in her deckchair and watched the others at work — Poppy was so excited about the play, she just wanted to make sure that everything was perfect!

"Edward, you've got to move *everything*," called Poppy.
The others looked up from what they were doing, then they looked at each other.

"Do it yourself, Princess Bossy Boots!" said Edward.
"Poppy, you are giving us an awful lot of orders," noticed Daisy.
"And you're not doing anything," said Honey.

"That's not true, I'm organizing the whole play," explained Poppy. "It's my garden, so it's my play, and you have to do what I say."

"This isn't fun any more," said Honey. "I'm going home."

"I know, let's do the play in Honey's garden," suggested Edward.

Everyone except Poppy thought this was a brilliant idea, so they gathered everything they needed and headed off to Honey's, leaving Poppy all on her own.

Poppy stormed inside, ran to the playroom and threw herself onto the beanbag. Hot tears pricked her eyes.

"What's the matter?" asked Mum.

"Nobody likes me," wailed Poppy. "They've gone to Honey's without me, and all because of the stupid play."

"Do you really think it's just about the play," asked Mum, "or about you?"

"Maybe a bit about me," said Poppy, sitting up and sniffing. "I was quite bossy, but only because I wanted everything to be perfect. I still want to be in the play, but I don't think they'll let me — what am I going to do?"

"What do *you* think you should do?" asked Mum as she stroked Poppy's hair.

"Say sorry?" said Poppy, knowing in her heart that it was the right thing to do.

Poppy felt fluttery inside as she walked towards Honeypot Cottage.

What if no one will speak to me?

Poppy pushed the gate open and they all turned to look at her.

"I'm really, really sorry for being so bossy and horrible and selfish. Please can I be in your play – I promise I'll do what I'm told," said Poppy before anyone else had a chance to say anything.

"Come on then," said Daisy. "You can help us finish the tickets."

"And *you* have to clear away your own toys," laughed Edward.

"All right then," agreed Poppy, just pleased to be friends again.

When the tickets were done they picked up everything
they needed for the play and went back to Poppy's garden.

"Ah, perfect timing," said Grandpa. "I've just finished the story."

"What's it called?" asked Honey.

"*Princess Bossy Boots!*" replied Grandpa. Everyone laughed – even Poppy.

"And who am I?" asked Edward.

"The wizard, of course," said Grandpa.

"And Mum's going to be the Fairy Godmother."

Poppy arranged the
chairs on the lawn

and Honey set off round the
village to deliver the tickets.

Daisy got the
costumes ready

and Edward finished
clearing the garden.

They waited for Honey to get back, and after a few dress rehearsals, they were ready. The audience started arriving. They took their seats and waited for the performance to begin – just like in a real theatre!

Daisy, Poppy and Honey walked onto the 'stage' in their gorgeous costumes and Grandpa told the story.

One day Princess Poppy and Princess Honey Blossom were having tea in the palace garden with their mother, Queen Daisy. Everything was peaceful and they were all very happy. Then suddenly, the sky darkened and there was an icy chill in the air . . . the wicked wizard had returned . . .

Edward swept onto the stage, pulling his cloak around him. "Ha-ha," he cackled as he threw magic bossy dust towards the little princesses, "you won't be so perfect now . . ."

The dust missed Honey Blossom, but Poppy was covered. From that moment on, Poppy became the horriblest, bossiest, most selfish princess ever, and everyone called her Princess Bossy Boots. As time passed, Poppy grew sadder and lonelier, but also bossier and more selfish.

The Queen and Princess Honey Blossom missed the old Poppy desperately and they searched far and wide for someone who could cast a spell to bring her back. A whole year went by, then, just as they were about to give up hope, Princess Poppy's Fairy Godmother appeared . . .

Mum fluttered onto the stage, wearing a beautiful silver dress and shimmering fairy wings. She sprinkled a magical rose petal potion over Poppy and waved her fairy wand.

"Goodbye, Princess Bossy Boots!" she chanted.

At last, the old Poppy was back! Poppy, Honey Blossom
and Queen Daisy locked the wicked wizard in the tower,
threw away the key and lived happily ever after . . .

The audience clapped and cheered as Poppy, Honey, Daisy, Edward, Grandpa and Mum held hands and took their bow. What a great team they were.

"I loved being a princess in the play," said Poppy. "I wish I could be a princess all the time."

"Yeah, but you can only be a princess if you're not bossy and selfish, and you know what you're like!" joked Edward.

They all laughed, even Poppy, but she had learned her lesson that day. She promised herself that she would try to be nicer to her friends and family and not quite so bossy.